Bird Woman

Written and Illustrated by Jan Atamian

*Dedicated to the Free Spirits
of the world*

Bird Woman

A long time ago, there lived a woman with golden eyes, smooth olive skin, and the feathery white body of a dove.

Wherever she flew, she always left a trail of forest pine smoke and cherry pie. People looked up to the skies and called her "Bird Woman."

Day in and day out, Bird Woman flew elegantly through endless changes in wind and clouds, from misty vapors to rolling thunder.

She gazed down onto the earth, observing
the tiny speck-like villages, green and abundant
with life. She observed how the tiny people scur-
ried about in the sunlight. When darkness fell,
she imagined pleasant conversations around the
hearth of an open fire.

It was a tiresome life, for Bird Woman, as she was always reflecting upon how others lived, and always feeling unsettled or embodied in wanderlust. Bird Woman had never known the company of other creatures, for she was born in a legend, emerging quietly from a shiny spiral conch shell. It was al-ready written that she would live a life of uncertain destination.

On a clear summer day, a faint sound from a distant flute lingers in the air. The ancient sound twirls and swirls upwards into the sky, before fading into the horizon. Bird Woman feels a sense of intrigue while listening to the magical music. Her heart screams out into the tranquil atmosphere. It palpitates rapidly as she exclaims, "I will defy these written laws. I will change my destiny!"

Upon hearing her words, the skies become still. Then opening up to crackling thunder, golden bolts of lightning from a dark cloud hurl out towards her feathery wings.

Off in the distance, the faint notes of a lone viola float upward, surrounding Bird Woman. The notes guide her wings down, bringing her closer to the tiny village.

Now it just so happens that down below on the highest hilltop a celebration of enormous proportion is taking place among the ruins of an ancient temple by the tranquility of the Aegean Sea. A young maiden, adorned in the flowers and herbs of the countryside and dressed in the purest white linen, stands in the center of a great mass of fallen stones.

Tears roll down her smooth olive skin, becoming trapped in a hollowed place in the hillside. It is the day of her wedding where without question, without defiance, she will be united with a dark stranger she has never seen or smelled before.

Bird Woman flies closer to the crowd on the hilltop. Tiny doves surrounding her feet coo. A delighted child holding a bouquet of fragrant orchids points up to the sky and cries, "Look Mama, it's an angel from the heavens!"

Bird Woman calmly flies down and descends upon the tiny white-washed village. Scooping up the sad maiden who smells of wild thyme and lavender, Bird Woman continues to fly steadily upward with confidence. Circling over misty vapors, the two travel through clouds shaped like endless wishes and dreams.

Closing her wings, Bird Woman lands and places the maiden safely on the shores of a sandy beach. Quietly, Bird Woman watches the waves from the blue-green sea caress the land, a land she has only imagined walking upon.

It is here that Bird Woman decides to stay, living out the remainder of her life in a tiny white-washed house by the Aegean, topped with a cerulean-blue roof.

The young maiden soon falls in love with a
shepherd who plays a beautiful horn while tending
to his flock of sheep. At the bottom of a green
mountain, surrounded by fields of richly colored
wildflowers, they build a house of stone and
live happily.

Bird Woman cares for her doves, listening to them coo and sing from a terrace overlooking the sea. It is here she dies, a contented old woman who no longer needs to wander or fly.

ABOUT THE AUTHOR

Jan Atamian studied painting, drawing and illustration at Syracuse University and received a master's degree in art education from the University of Massachusetts–Amherst.

She has worked as a muralist painter in Nicaragua, as an art teacher in urban public schools, a counselor facilitating art groups for adolescents in community mental health, and at a community homeless shelter.

Bird Woman, a mythological creature in ancient myth, lived around the Euphrates River, which originated in the Armenian Highlands of eastern Turkey. Jan created fabric collage art to illustrate this magical tale.